Rex

Ursula Dubosarsky

Illustrated by David Mackintosh

A Neal Porter Book
Roaring Brook Press
New Milford, Connecticut

For the fabulous Shrubb family—U. D. • For Ruby Middleton and Tierry D'Actil—D. M.
Text copyright © 2005 by Ursula Dubosarsky, Illustrations copyright © 2005 by David Mackintosh

A Neal Porter Book, Published by Roaring Brook Press
Roaring Brook Press is a division of Holtzbrinck Publishing Holdings Limited Partnership, 143 West Street, New Milford, Connecticut 06776

First published in Australia by The Penguin Group

Library of Congress Cataloging-in-Publication Data
Dubosarsky, Ursula, 1961-
Rex / Ursula Dubosarsky; illustrated by David Mackintosh.—1st American ed.
p. cm.
"A Neal Porter book."
Summary: Students take turns bringing home the class chameleon and writing about how he spent his visit.
ISBN-13: 978-1-59643-186-7 / ISBN-10: 1-59643-186-5
[1. Chameleons as pets--Fiction. 2. Pets--Fiction. 3. Schools--Fiction.] I. Mackintosh, David, ill. II. Title.
PZ7.D8529Re 2006 [E]--dc22 2005033744

Roaring Brook Press books are available for special promotions and premiums. For details, contact: Director of Special Markets, Holtzbrinck Publishers.

Printed in China

First American edition August 2006

10 9 8 7 6 5 4 3 2 1

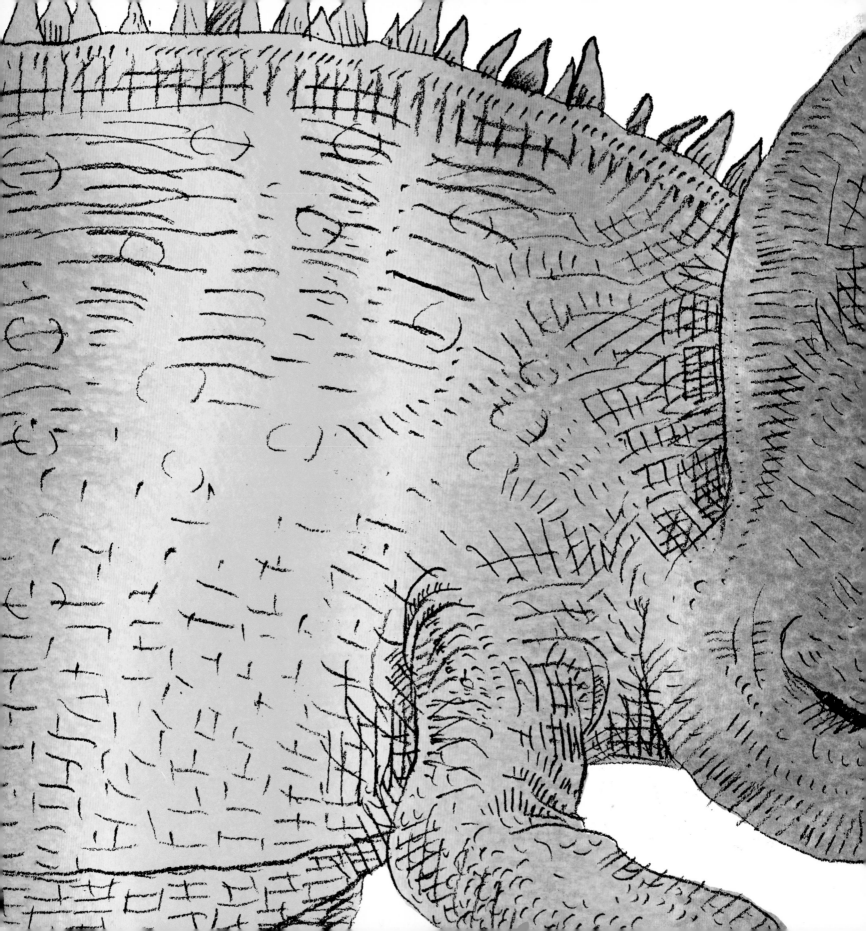

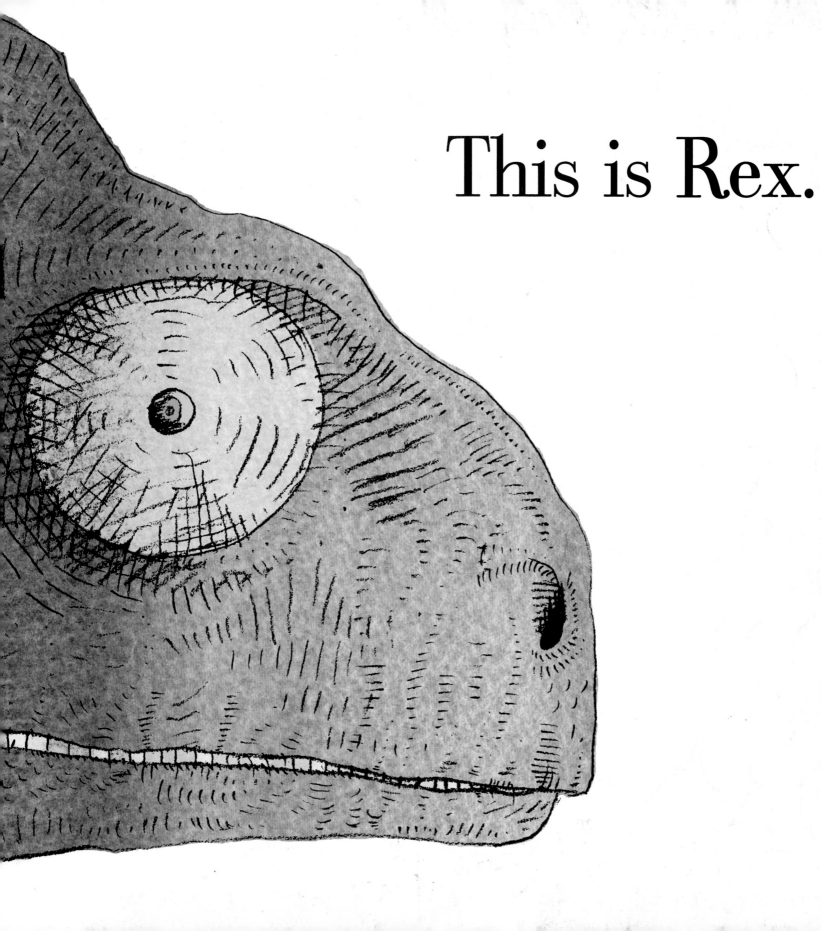

This is Rex.

Rex is our class pet.

Every day, someone
gets to take Rex home.

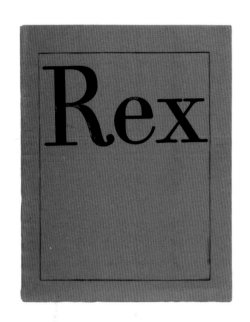  

You take Rex home with a special book.

  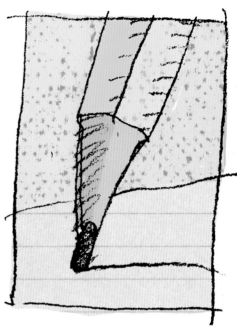

In the special book, you write
all the things Rex did on his visit.

If you can't write,

...you can
draw a picture.

On Monday, Rex went home with Jai.

Jai has a swimming pool.
Rex went for a swim.

Lucky he can float.

On Tuesday, Hilary took Rex home.
Hilary lives in a big apartment building.

Rex fell out
the window.

He was a bit surprised,
but at least nobody
was underneath.

On Wednesday, Sam took Rex home.
Rex helped Sam's mom in the shop.

Some of the customers got scared. Rex is used to that.

On Thursday, Amy took Rex home.

Amy has a little brother.

He dressed Rex up in Malibu Barbie's clothes.
It's a good thing Rex has a sense of humor.

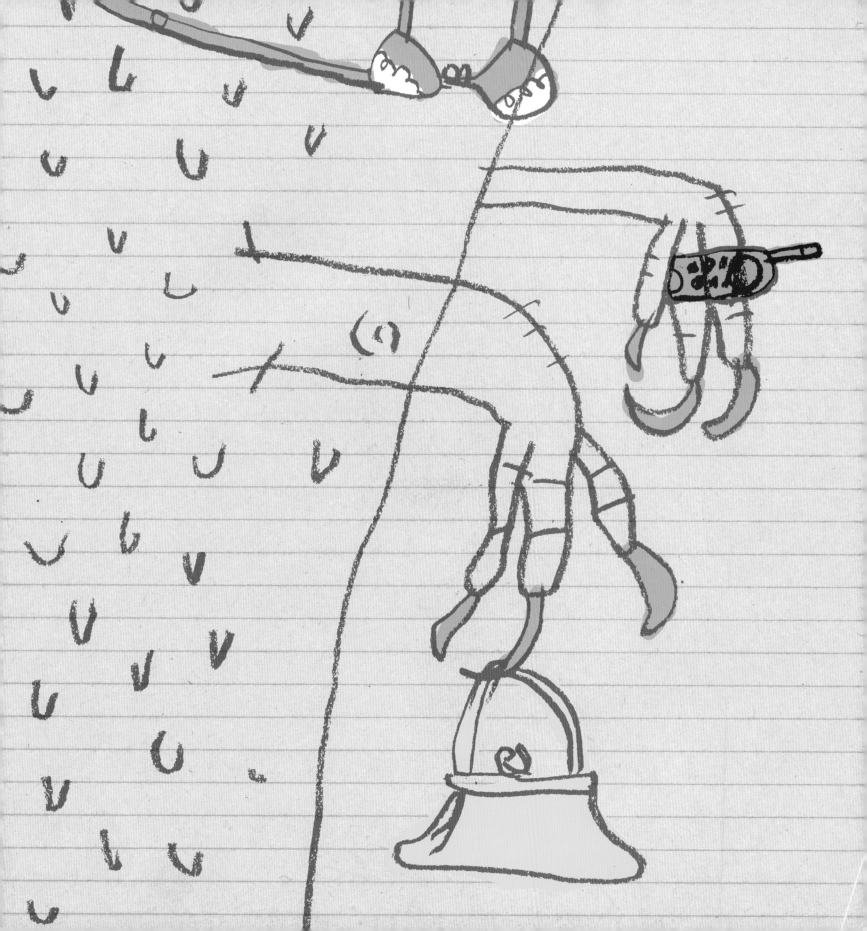

Now it's Friday.
At last it's my turn!

I'm lucky. I can have Rex for the whole weekend.
I wonder what I will do with Rex?

Maybe we will go to the movies.
What sort of movie would Rex like?

Or to a restaurant.
Would Rex like a giant hamburger?

Maybe we will hide behind
the door and jump out
when someone goes by.

AAAAAAAA AAAAAAAAA AAGGGGH HHH!

Then, when we are tired, we will snuggle up under the blankets and go to sleep.

I wonder if Rex snores?

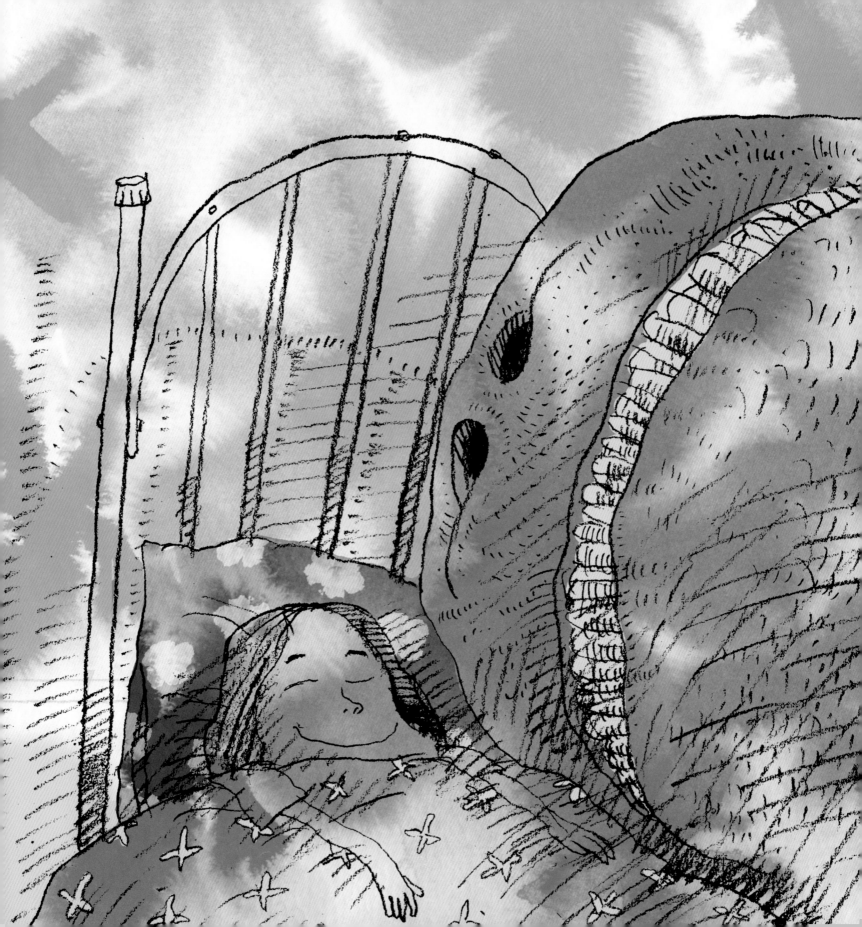

I love Rex.
What would *you* do if Rex came to visit *you*?